I0741955

Don't do it Johnny

By Adam Khedoori

Dedications and Gratitude
Thank you readers!

Thank you for investing in the future.
Thanks to my wife and role models, who help me make life wonderful.
Thanks to my children who give me inspiration to improve myself. Thank you to my wonderful family who has given me so much. Thanks to all who helped make this book possible. Thanks to the great teachers of this world who are here to guide us! Thanks Creator for giving us life!

Copyright © 2020 Adam Khedoori

Book: ISBN - 978-0-6488457-7-5

First published 2020 by Think and Grow Publishing © Sydney, Australia

Authored by **Adam Khedoori (Australia)**
Edited by **Renee Kurz (Australia), Zahara Francisco (Philippines), Kathy Beckman (USA), Adam Khedoori (Australia), Anita Khedoori**

Illustrations by **Prabir Sarkar (India)**
Layout by **Kashif Tahir (Pakistan)**

www.thinkgrowpublish.com

Inspiration quotes the seeds of success

"A good quote can sink into the heart and plant a seed and bring out our best qualities. Think about one a day and make your mind shine!" **Adam Khedoori**

"If you are willing to do only what's easy, life will be hard. But if you're willing to do what's hard, life will be easy." **T. Harv Eker**

"Whether you think you can, or you think you can't- You're right." **Henry Ford**

"Formal education will make you a living, self-education will make you a fortune."
"If you really want to do something, you'll find a way. If you don't, you'll find an excuse." **Jim Rohn**

"We cannot always build a future for our youth, but we can always build our youth for the future." **Franklin D. Roosevelt**

"When educating the minds of our youth, we must not forget to educate their hearts." **Dalai Lama**

"The youth is the hope of our future." **Jose Rizal**

"Whatever the mind can conceive and believe, the mind can achieve."
Napoleon Hill

"When we are no longer able to change a situation, we are challenged to change ourselves."
"Everything can be taken from a person but one thing: the last of the human freedoms-to choose one's attitude in any given set of circumstances, to choose one's own way."
"Between stimulus and response there is a space. In that space is our power to choose our response. In our response lies our growth and our freedom."
Viktor Frankl

One morning, Johnny was in the
bathroom getting ready for school.
His Mother called out,
"Johnny, brush your teeth!"
Johnny didn't brush his teeth.

After school, Johnny and his mum went to the park. His mum warned, "Johnny, please play safely, and be careful on that slide!"
Johnny didn't listen again. He was jumping and playing so roughly that he fell on his arm and scratched it all up.

Later, Mum and Johnny were outside in the backyard. Mum instructed Johnny, "Johnny, the dog is bored. Please play a quiet game with the dog. But do not play anything that will make the dog bark loudly as the neighbor is taking a nap."

Johnny didn't listen to his mum's instructions. Instead, he ran around the backyard with the dog chasing and barking at him.

At the dinner table, mum cut up
some delicious fruit for Johnny.
Mum said, "Johnny, eat some fruit.
It's good for you."
Johnny didn't eat the fruit.
Instead, he pushed them aside in
disgust saying, "YUCK!"

After dinner, the family was relaxing in the living room. Mum and Dad were reading, Johnny was playing video games and his sister was complaining that she was bored. "Won't you let your sister play the video game with you?" Mum pleaded with Johnny. Johnny didn't listen to his mum's request, so his sister got angry and unplugged his game.

Getting ready for bed his mum gave him one final chore. "Johnny, pick up your clothes and put them in the laundry basket." She said. Again, Johnny disobeyed his mum. He even removed the clothes he was wearing and threw them on the floor!

Mum was getting confused and very frustrated. She loved Johnny so much! And wanted him to listen to her. But how?
Suddenly, Mum had an idea. She would trick Johnny by saying the opposite of what she wants him to do!

Would this work?
She was going to find out.

The next morning, Johnny was in the bathroom, getting ready for school. His mum called out, "Johnny, DON'T brush your teeth!" Mum called out. But Johnny DID brush his teeth!

After school, Johnny and his mum went to the park.
His mum warned him, "Johnny, DON'T play safely and
DON'T be careful on that slide!" Johnny DID the
opposite. He jumped and played safely.

Later, Mum and Johnny were in the backyard. Mum instructed Johnny, "Johnny, the dog is bored. Please DON'T play a quietly with the dog. Please let him chase you and bark loudly so that you can wake the neighbor from his nap!" But Johnny DID! He played a quiet game of fetch with the dog and had a wonderful time!

At the dinner table, Mum cut up some delicious fruit and placed it on Johnny's plate. Mum told him, "Johnny, DON'T eat fruit, It is NO good for you!" Johnny DID eat the fruit and learned that he actually liked it!

Johnny was playing with his video game, and his sister was sitting on the couch complaining that she was bored...again. Mum acting annoyed, told Johnny, "Definitely, DON'T share your video game with your sister!" But Johnny DID! He shared his video game with his sister and had the best time playing together!

Do you think Johnny was starting to understand that his mum was tricking him?

At the end of the evening, it was time for Johnny to get ready for bed. Mum commanded firmly, "Johnny, DON'T pick up your clothes and DON'T EVEN THINK ABOUT putting them in the laundry basket!" Not bothered by the stern tone of her voice, Johnny DID it. He put the clothes that were scattered all over the floor into the laundry basket. And, when he changed into his pajamas, he put his worn clothes into the laundry basket too!

What a strange turn of events! Mum could not believe it. Everything that she told Johnny NOT to do, Johnny DID!

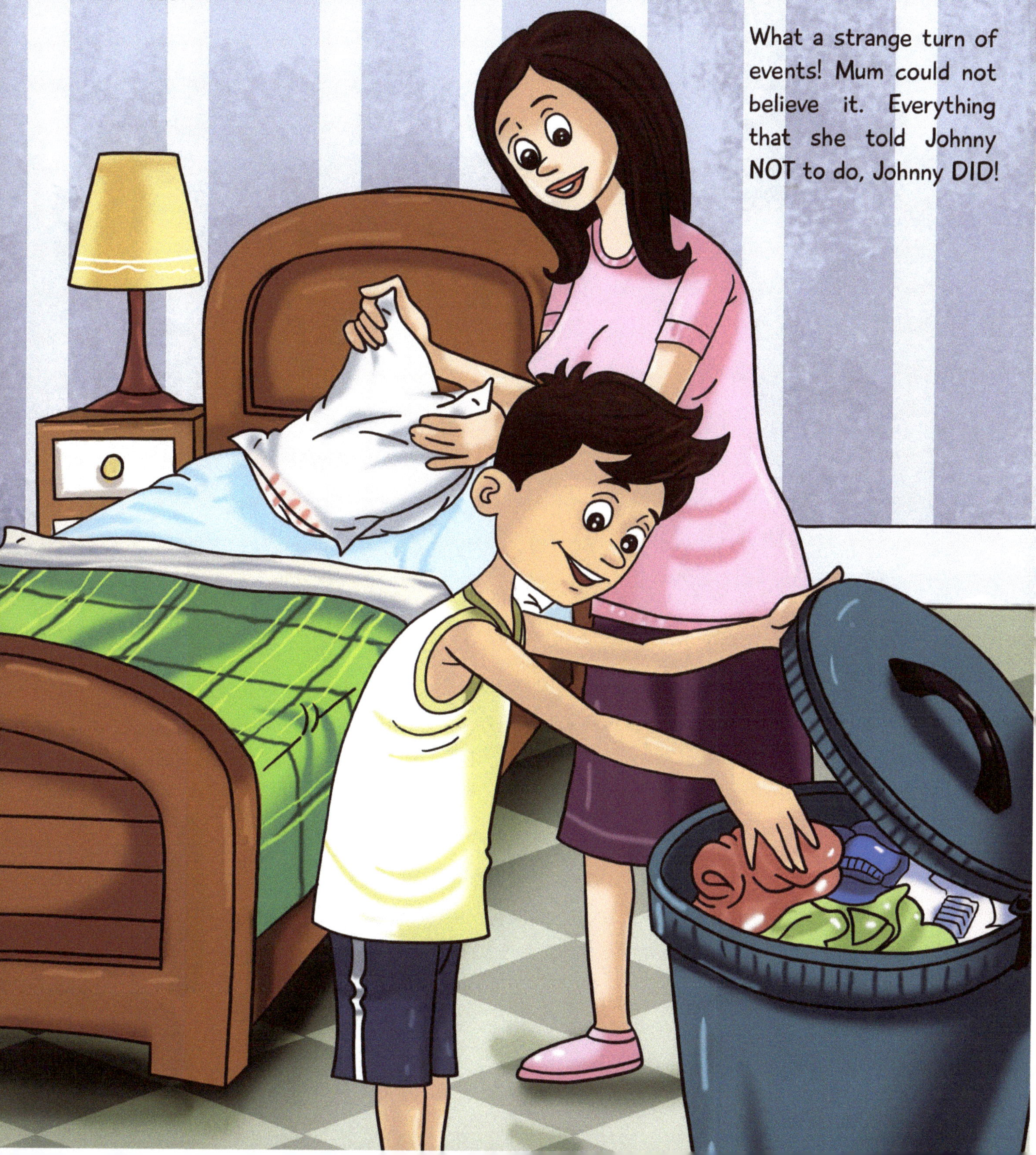

Out of curiosity, Mum asked Johnny, "What is it that you DON'T WANT to do?" Johnny replied with a smile, "Anything that you WANT me to do!" They both had a good laugh at Johnny's honest remark.

Finally, Johnny said to his mum sincerely, "Mum, I will listen to you more and do what you say because I had such a good time playing the opposite game!"

The end

About the Author

'Adam Khedoori'

Adam spent many years on a quest to find great teachers in this world and share their work.

He's an author, a publisher, and co-partner to LeRoy Malouf to present the Positive Power of Being Neutral (PPBN) Udemy©
www.udemy.com

He works as a healer at: www.clearlifenow.com

Adam's goal is to share his findings through picture books for the youth, parents and educators to learn how they can all develop a mind of self-growth and succeed in life, through the study of great people. Adam lives happily in Sydney, Australia with his wife, Anita and their 3 boys.

Follow **Think and Grow Publishing** on
Facebook: @DreamBelieveCreate2020
www.thinkgrowpublish.com

Introduction to Thought Leader Series

Dear readers,

Welcome to **Think and Grow Publishing's** first set of books.

These books are a little different so I would like to point out how you can get the most from reading them. My books are intended to provide parents, care-givers, educators and children, mental and emotional nutrition for fostering growth, happiness, and success in life.

The motto is:　　　　　**Dream it, Believe it and Create it**

Each book is planting seeds that will be able to sprout given the right efforts and a **Think and Grow formula.**

• **Dream:**　Think deeply about what you want to achieve. Be positive and do not state things in a negative way, don't see things worse than they are. Instead, try to see things clearly and without judgment. Dream how you want it to be. 'See things being on the way, not in the way', by Dr.John Demartini

• **Believe:**　Feel joy in your heart. When you have a goal to improve yourself or make life better for others, then your dream becomes aligned with 'making life wonderful' as Dr Marshall Rosenberg says is the purpose of life. You will have the energy to learn and develop yourself, 'You can be the person you can become' says Ryuho Okawa.

• **Create:** Take action to realize your dream. It requires patience, love, self-reflection, continual learning, change, and determination. Yes, life can be wonderful when you take just a little time each day to fill it up with the joy of self-improvement. Remember to just take one step at a time, and even if set-backs occur, keep searching and going forward.

About the style of this book and how you can get the best use out of it...

Firstly, there is an illustrated story with a message and ways to be happy, I have spent many years finding the root causes of problems in life and found a few hints for success and progress. Just like Bill Phillips said, "Focus on progress, not perfection."

Secondly, I introduce you to a thought leader who has found a way to make life wonderful in an area of life.

Thirdly, I will write a life changing essay in each book.

And finally, I share comments about the work of the thought leader and some basic principles.

Most importantly, I wish you to enjoy the experience and naturally sprout seeds in the garden of you and your children's minds. I hope that these books become the fertilizer to start a life of self-development, gratitude, and joyful living. You can create a magnificent garden in your mind!

With all my love.
Adam David Khedoori

Think and grow publishing values

Our values create our stories and drive us towards our goals. Values determine our actions and what we are doing right now.

Effort Make no effort is to make no progress.

Desire Hunger towards achieving success.

Progress Knowing the final goals, not about perfection it's about progress.

Resilience The noun resilience stems from the Latin resilience "to rebound, recoil." Resilience is a person's mental ability to recover quickly from misfortune, illness or depression and bounce back.

Courage The axe in your tool belt to cut down the physical, mental and emotional walls blocking the path, that leads to growth and progress.

Happiness The goal of life, knowing values and actions to make life wonderful, having a mind of giving, understanding the laws of cause and effect on mind.

Adversity Trials and tests that are here to support us and make us stronger.

Strength A capacity to know our limits and push through them, linked with progress, resilience, and courage.

Love Love means to give without expecting anything in return, When we do things from a loving place and not to "get", we find that love flows.

Forgiveness Forgiving ourselves or others from mistakes and learning from them.

Growth An inevitable part of life, we can stagnate, get complacent or we can choose growth and find joy in learning and developing ourselves.

Self reflection A chance to undo the past, make peace, and re-align with our goals of progress. We can change how we feel about an event or a person by thinking of the meaning behind it. It's not always about what happened, it's about how we feel about it.

Self-help spirit The spirit to take responsibility for our life, learning and opportunities. The feeling of pride in our own efforts.

Responsibility Acting in response to a cause and the ability to return to love, support, strength and progress.

Gratitude Gratitude means to be thankful for all that we have been given. Even for small things we can feel grateful for. Take 5 mins a day to think about things that help you.

Self-discipline One of the most important skills we need to master in order to accomplish anything in life. The ability to do what you need to do, when it needs to be done, whether you like it or not. This is biggest key to opening a door to our success.

If you are willing to do only what's easy, life will be hard. But if you are willing to do what's hard, life will be easy.

T. Harv Eker

Life Changing Essay
The Joy of Learning and Making Progress

Children are curious about everything. They gain knowledge of the world around them through tasting, touching, smelling, hearing, and watching. There are new foods to taste, new games to play, new people to meet, new things to wonder about and new concepts to learn every day. Children and adults feel joy when they learn because when they learn, they grow.

Learning to walk is a perfect example of this idea. Imagine a 12-month old baby of its own free will, strength and determination, trying with all his might to stand, and then cautiously gain his balance and walk. The baby pulls himself up and reaches for things to hold on to, and steady himself. The baby wobbles from side to side as his legs acclimate to this new, exciting motion. With practice, his leg muscles strengthen, he develops balance, and he gains the confidence to move forward on his own. He is soon tottering into the loving arms of his parents, albeit hesitantly.

Throughout this process, no one has said to the baby, "You can't walk. You will never be able to walk!" This is nonsensical thinking that goes against the baby's natural progression of development.

The baby's parents, relatives, and friends encourage and support him to walk and develop, transitioning from infancy to toddlerhood. The term "toddler" is derived from the phrase "to toddle," which means to walk unsteadily. So, before one can walk with joy and grace, one must experience this part of development. It will not always be smooth, but with persistence, courage, and a curiosity of the unknown, one will be equipped to walk through life's journey with joy and grace.

In all our thinking, we must understand and value… Explore these ideas in your work or classrooms.

- A love of learning
- The joy of learning
- A passion for learning
- A life-long learning spirit
- Self-discipline

- Learning not as a means to an end, but as an end in and of itself
- Higher development
- Learning is fun

- CANI - Constant And Never-ending Improvement
- Goals and a mission statement

The most critical key to learning has two sides. These are very powerful to know about and will change our thinking for the better.

- **One is a willingness to learn,** meaning how willing is a person to learn something new, maybe they say they already know that, but they don't actually know enough about it to use it to add value and apply

- **Two is a willingness to change,** once you learn something new, do you dismiss it and never think about it again? Do you think negatively first about it? Are you willing to change when you learn new things?

The big key here is to have a passion for learning. By developing a curious nature and not being afraid to say, "I don't understand" or "I didn't quite get that" and feel okay with it. Don't join the crowds of complacency and get stuck in the habit of losing this passionate nature in your studies or education. So, Ask questions and raise your hand when you don't quite understand something.

Do you remember the joy of learning to walk and explore? There is a joy to learning and improving oneself that brings about happiness. Happiness and development are one and the same. For that reason, foster the joy of learning and achieve happiness.

Adam Khedoori

Dr Joseph Murphy - Modern Day Thought Leader

The master key to success in life
Power of habits and subconscious mind

Everyone needs to dream. A life without dreams is a life without hope. **Master Ryuho Okawa, from "The Laws of the Sun"**

Before I started this topic I wanted to point out that Dr Murphy's book is full of incredible information that will make your life more magical. I urge you to read it or listen to his audiobooks on Youtube.

Learning how to use your subconscious mind will help you to be successful, have harmonious relationships with others, how to remove mental blocks, and fear from life, forgive yourself and others, and get the things you want in life. Dr Joseph Murphy explains how to use the power of the mind to become an electromagnet for the things you want. With his most famous book called **The Subconscious Mind**, he outlines the step by step process in making dreams come true which may look like miracles happening in one's life.

In the book, Murphy explains how he healed himself, and explains that you don't know the full power of our mind until you experience miraculous healing in your body. He says, **"Many years ago I managed to cure myself of a malignancy - in medical terminology it is called a sarcoma - by using the healing power of my subconscious mind, which created me and still maintains and governs all my vital functions."**

You see the mind is made of two parts, one is the conscious and the other is the subconscious mind. The conscious mind is the one that we can hear when we think, we can have only one thought at a time. While the subconscious mind is a warehouse of our thoughts and memories. It even determines our personality and how we think and look at the world.

A metaphor that clearly shows the mind and subconscious mind is based on an iceberg. An Iceberg is only visible from the surface of the water; you can see only about 10% of it, however, 90% is hidden beneath the surface. So the top is conscious and the bottom is subconscious. We all know what happened to the Titanic ship, Can you imagine an iceberg that can conquer a ship?

So if you want to understand the mind in a greater sense you can see that when the bottom is strong and filled with the right information and programs, it becomes unstoppable.

Many people fail in losing fat or dieting, why is that? Because their subconscious mind was not changed and they end up yo-yo-ing up and down.

To explain more about the mind, our beliefs drive our behavior. One of my favorite authors is James Allen who said: **"The outer conditions of a person's life will always reflect their inner beliefs."** I think you are starting to get the drift of how people are in control of their thinking and feelings, as we are not always able to control our environments, where we are born and how other people will treat and respond to us. So by understanding the subconscious mind and what's deeply in our programming of it. You could also look at the values page in this book and see that these values are also inside our subconscious mind just waiting for us to use them.

The thoughts in our subconscious are also made up of our life's experiences that we have learned from others and society. Dr Murphy explains that it can be reprogrammed, perhaps he was talking about the science we now know as neuroplasticity, where the brain changes shape according to our thinking and habits.

Your life is what your thoughts make it.
Confucius

Provided you are open-minded and receptive, the infinite intelligence within your subconscious mind can reveal to you everything you need to know at every moment of time and point of space. You can receive new thoughts and ideas, bring forth new inventions, make discoveries, create new works of art. The infinite intelligence in your subconscious can give you access to wonderful new kinds of knowledge. Let it reveal itself to you and it will open the way to perfect expression and true place in your life. The infinite intelligence in your subconscious can give you access to wonderful new kinds of knowledge. Let it reveal itself to you and it will open the way to perfect expression and true place in your life." "The principles of chemistry, physics, and mathematics are no different in their workings from the principles of your subconscious mind. **Dr Joseph Murphy, Excerpt from the book, "The Subconscious Mind"**

Murphy explains that first we need to get ourselves into the relaxed state which is a big factor in directing our mind to focus on the things we want to create in life. To focus deeply, we need to hold a thought for some time without any opposing thoughts that are being blown around inside our heads all the time and block the outcome we desire.

Adam's method for quieting and , going through the layers of the mind and reaching the subconscious:

1. Sit comfortably, take a few gentle deep breaths into your belly, and calm yourself down. Become aware of your mind producing thoughts without engaging with them. If you find yourself getting engaged with the thought, take a moment to acknowledge them and return to breathing. (you may write down repeated thoughts on paper or things you need to add to your to-do list.)

2. If certain thoughts produce strong emotions in you, feel the emotions instead of trying to suppress the thoughts. Divert your attention within your body and feel the energy behind these thoughts.

3. If you have any thoughts repeating or ideas or things you need to remember, write them on paper.

4. As you watch your thoughts, you will become aware of many negative thought patterns running in you. Simply becoming aware of these patterns is enough for them to start disintegrating.

5. Counter all the negative thoughts and think an opposite positive to each one. Another optional step is to "Let go fully of anything deep inside of you that bothers you regularly" Maybe you can repeat "Don't sweat the little stuff, It's all little stuff."

How did you feel? Did you try it for a few minutes? Do you feel your mind calmer and body lighter? If you didn't get this on the first try then you can give it another go, you will get better each time you do it.

Do you have to believe in God? Murphy studied not only religious books but also disease and wellness. He found out that the power of believing that you will get better, you will succeed or just being happy is based on your belief. Before any religion, people had made a life and lived happily. They had belief, belief in something that was guiding them. So I urge you to look deep inside and believe in your divine power inside of you, some calling it God, Eternal Buddha, Divine or creative intelligence. Murphy says it is the single factor for your success, Belief.

> You have infinite riches within your reach
> **Dr Joseph Murphy**

Scientific Prayer, what is it? When you believe in an infinite power then your prayer is effective, A prayer stated in the positive of what you want. Note prayer can also mean spoken affirmation, which simply means impressing on your mind the very thing you want.

It's important to know in modern times we have a method of meditation called TM which stands for Transcendental Meditation. It's a method of repeating positive statements, a word or a sound for 10 minutes or more a day. The effects are incredible for avoiding distracting thoughts and promoting a state of relaxed awareness. So in short Murphy has worked out a similar formula that is effective in any age of humankind to change the subconscious mind.

Your subconscious accepts any ideas you repeatedly think about which psychologists and psychotherapists agreed is true.

Murphy's book is full of testimonials about how people improved their lives and used this powerful force within their minds.

A short excerpt from the book The Subconscious mind.

HAVE YOU ACCEPTED ANY OF THESE?

From the day we are born, we are bombarded with negative suggestions. Not knowing how to counter them, we unconsciously accept them and bring them into being as our experience.

Here are some examples of negative suggestions:

You can't
You mustn't
It's no use
There's no point in
trying so hard
Life is an endless
grind

You'll never amount
to anything
You haven't got a
chance
It's not what you
know, but who you
know
You're too old now
You just can't win

You'll fail
You're all wrong
What's the use,
nobody cares
Things are getting
worse and worse
Watch out, you'll
catch a terrible
disease

Check your mind thoroughly if you have accepted any of these negative suggestions when your mind is in a calm and relaxed state. If you find yourself thinking negatively, it's possible to replace them immediately by thinking the opposite of these thoughts. He says, "You may take a few times but once you change any negative thoughts around you, you will find a natural joy coming from your heart."

 The fundamental cause of distress or anxiety in life is the belief that your happiness is dependent on outside factors.
"An Unshakable Mind" by Master Ryuho Okawa

These very statements may be inside our minds, that block us from our full potential. The subconscious mind can block or enable us to reach our goals and dreams.

After examining Murphy's work it becomes clear to see that our thoughts are being realised. What we can do with the power of the mind by repeatedly focusing on positive outcomes and feelings we will manifest.

Our subconscious mind can also be our thinking habits. Also called mindset is the direction our mind thinks in and is made of habitual thinking. These are our routines and behavior that are repeated regularly and tend to occur subconsciously. The American Journal of Psychology defines a "habit, from the standpoint of psychology, [as] a more or less fixed way of thinking, willing, or feeling acquired through previous repetition of a mental experience."

Another key to your success

What is the most important habit? Brain Tracy explains in his book called Self-discipline "You don't need to have been born under a lucky star, or with incredible wealth, or with terrific contacts and connections, or even special skills but what you do need to succeed in any of your life goals is self-discipline." Brian also mentions in his work jokingly that fortunately, anyone can learn good habits. Everyone has an opportunity to develop and learn.

Murphy explains that the mind is the central part and it is quite important for us to access and change our minds in a positive direction.

Watch your thoughts, they become your words; watch your words, they become your actions; watch your actions, they become your habits; watch your habits, they become your character, watch your character, it becomes your destiny. **Lao Tzu**

Basis of the laws of cause and effect

To understand another way under the laws of cause and effect, which states all things come from a cause and the result is the effect. From my research and own experience, many people live on the side of reacting in the state of effect, a type of victim mentality. This internally sounds like "You did this to me" or "this is because of you" it's a kind of blame, that others cause you to feel disconnected. You must live from a place of a cause which is a creative position. So much of our culture has been learned from our friends, family, peers, even social media has shaped our reactions and thinking. So we need to understand the fact that we can control our minds and become creators of what we wish to create in this world and for our lives.

You have always been thinking and causing things to happen in your life. So have you thought about your dreams and what you want in life?

"We become what we think about most of the time, and that's the strangest secret."
Earl Nightingale

What we do daily and our actions are based on what's in our subconscious mind. Joseph Murphy's classic book is still sold today called The subconscious mind. It is the foundation of how our thoughts lead to our actions. We can learn a lot about ourselves when we know what the difference is between the subconscious and the conscious mind. Our conscious mind is our voice inside our head, what we say and think. Note we can only think about one thought at a time, this being a factor as shown in people who have anxiety. When we become mindful about our thoughts, we can control our minds, rather than our thoughts that cause us to feel eg. anxious, alone, separate etc, or positive feelings of joy, calm, wellness and more.

The mind is a superpower, western science may show the mind is located in the brain, however eastern philosophy shows the mind is located around the heart. While the brain is a processor of the body, our heart in a study reacts before the brain.

Epigenetics is a study of genies and how they turn off and on and form DNA. What Bruce Lipton PhD discovered was that beliefs control human biology rather than DNA and inheritance. He worked on a megaproject called the Human Genome mapping out millions of DNA in a human being and worked out that there is a factor of thoughts that affect the turning on and off of certain genes.

"Never complain, never explain. Resist the temptation to defend yourself or make excuses."
"The ability to discipline yourself to delay gratification in the short to enjoy greater rewards in the long term is the indispensable prerequisite for success." **Brian Tracy**

I would suggest you all watch or listen to Dr Joseph Murphy's works on Youtube or get his audiobooks. His works are full of incredible information that will make your life more magical. Put these steps into action to create a life you want to live. Repeatedly listening can make it easier for you to grasp the full potential that lies deep in each of our minds, then realises it by actions.

Thank you,
Adam Khedoori

Murphy quotes to contemplate

"He awakened to the simple truth that it is never what a person says or does that affects him, it is his reaction to what is said or done that matters."

"All disease originates in the mind. Nothing appears on the body unless there is a mental pattern corresponding to it."

"There is no virtue in poverty."

Scientific prayer

"You can know that your prayer was successful by the feeling in your Heart that the worries and the fears have gone."

"The swimming instructor knows that if you lie still in the water you will float. But if you get nervous, tense, and fearful you will sink."

"A mind at peace always knows the answer."

All feedback is encouraged with gratitude!

Dear readers,

Thank you so much for taking the time to read and discover the great people featured in this book. I hope this story will assist and plant a seed in your child's mind for infinite growth and success in their future.

I would love to get your feedback, Positive I hope… if you have any ideas or criticism let me know directly via Feedback on www.goodreads.com search "Adam Khedoori" you will see all my books there and on Facebook page:
Facebook[@DreamBelieveCreate2020]

If you think this book is useful and helpful to your school, community, friends or family please share it with them. Our mission is to bring a bright future towards the world and make this world a wonderful place planting positive seeds one at a time.

Sending a big THANK YOU and letting you know I BELIEVE EVERYONE IS GOOD INSIDE!

www.ingramcontent.com/pod-product-compliance
Lightning Source LLC
Chambersburg PA
CBHW041202100726
47911CB00016B/824